Woolly the Bully

by Sue Graves

Illustrated by Tim Archbold

W

FRANKLIN WATTS
LONDON·SYDNEY

Woolly
the Bully

First published in 2007 by
Franklin Watts
338 Euston Road
London
NW1 3BH

Franklin Watts Australia
Level 17/207 Kent Street
Sydney
NSW 2000

A CIP catalogue record for this book is available
from the British Library.

ISBN 978 0 7496 7098 6 (hbk)
ISBN 978 0 7496 7790 9 (pbk)

Series Editor: Jackie Hamley
Editor: Melanie Palmer
Series Advisor: Dr Barrie Wade
Series Designer: Peter Scoulding

Printed in China

Franklin Watts is a division of
Hachette Children's Books,
an Hachette Livre UK company.

Woolly was a mammoth.
He was Rocky's
favourite pet.

But Woolly was a bully –
the worst that you can get.

He tripped up Mrs Pebble,
and made her spill the tea.

9

Then he frightened
Mr Pebble ...

Grrr!

and chased him up a tree!

Mr and Mrs Pebble
saw Rocky and his dad.

"We don't want bullies here," they said.

"He'll have to go.

He's bad!"

So sadly Rocky and his dad
sent Woolly on his way.

But Woolly hid behind
the cave.

He hoped that he could stay.

Later on there was
a thunderstorm.

It rained and rained
all night.

The rain filled up
the Pebbles'
cave.

It was a scary sight!

"HELP, HELP!" yelled
Mrs Pebble.

"We're stuck on a
water spout!"

Woolly heard them yelling.

He ran to get them out.

"Thanks Woolly," said Mr Pebble. "Please don't go away."

"We'd like you here forever. Please say that you will stay."

Now Woolly's back with Rocky. He's still his favourite pet.

Woolly never bullies now.
He's the best pet you
can get!

Leapfrog has been specially designed to fit the requirements of the National Literacy Strategy. It offers real books for beginning readers by top authors and illustrators. There are 67 Leapfrog stories to choose from:

* hardback